The Adventures of ARNiE the DOUGHNUT

BOWLING ALLEY BANDIT

written and illustrated by

LAURIE KELLER

SQUARE FISH

Henry Holt and Company — New York

This book is dedicated to my incredible editor, Christy Ottaviano

My heartfelt thanks to Jenny Whitehead, Charise Mericle Harper, Marissa Moss, Deb Pilutti, Jason Schneider, Carol Osborne, Patrick Regan, Lori Eslick, Charlie McCarthy, Amy Young, Scott Mack, and my mom for all your feedback and encouragement while making this book.

Thank you, Brad Jacobs, for the behind-the-scenes photo-shoot access at Northway Lanes, and to Marlaine Dempsey, second-grade teacher at Pine Crest School in Ft. Lauderdale, Florida, for the "Who Don-ut Mystery" pun on the cover.

Thank you, George Wen and Marianne Cohen, for always promptly and kindly answering my never-ending punctuation questions.

And thank you as always to Christy Ottaviano and April Ward for all your hard work making this book come together.

SQUARE FISH

An Imprint of Macmillan
175 Fifth Avenue
New York, NY 10010
mackids.com

Square Fish books may be purchased for business or promotional use. For information
on bulk purchases, please contact the Macmillan Corporate and Premium Sales Department
at (800) 221-7945 x5442 or by e-mail at specialmarkets@macmillan.com.

Library of Congress Cataloging-in-Publication Data
Keller, Laurie.
Bowling alley bandit / written and illustrated by Laurie Keller.
p.   cm. — (The adventures of Arnie the Doughnut ; [1])
Summary: Arnie the talking doughnut is delighted to be Mr. Bing's new pet
"doughnut-dog," so when Mr. Bing starts rolling gutter balls during a big bowling
tournament, Arnie suspects foul play and sets out to solve the mystery.
ISBN 978-1-250-07249-8 (paperback)
[1. Doughnuts—Fiction. 2. Bowling—Fiction.
3. Mystery and detective stories. 4. Humorous stories.] I. Title.
PZ7.K281346Bow 2013   [Fic]—dc23   2012028113

Originally published in the United States by
Christy Ottaviano Books/Henry Holt and Company
First Square Fish Edition: 2015
Square Fish logo designed by Filómena Tuosto

10 9 8 7 6 5

AR: 3.6 / LEXILE: 690L

CHAPTER 1

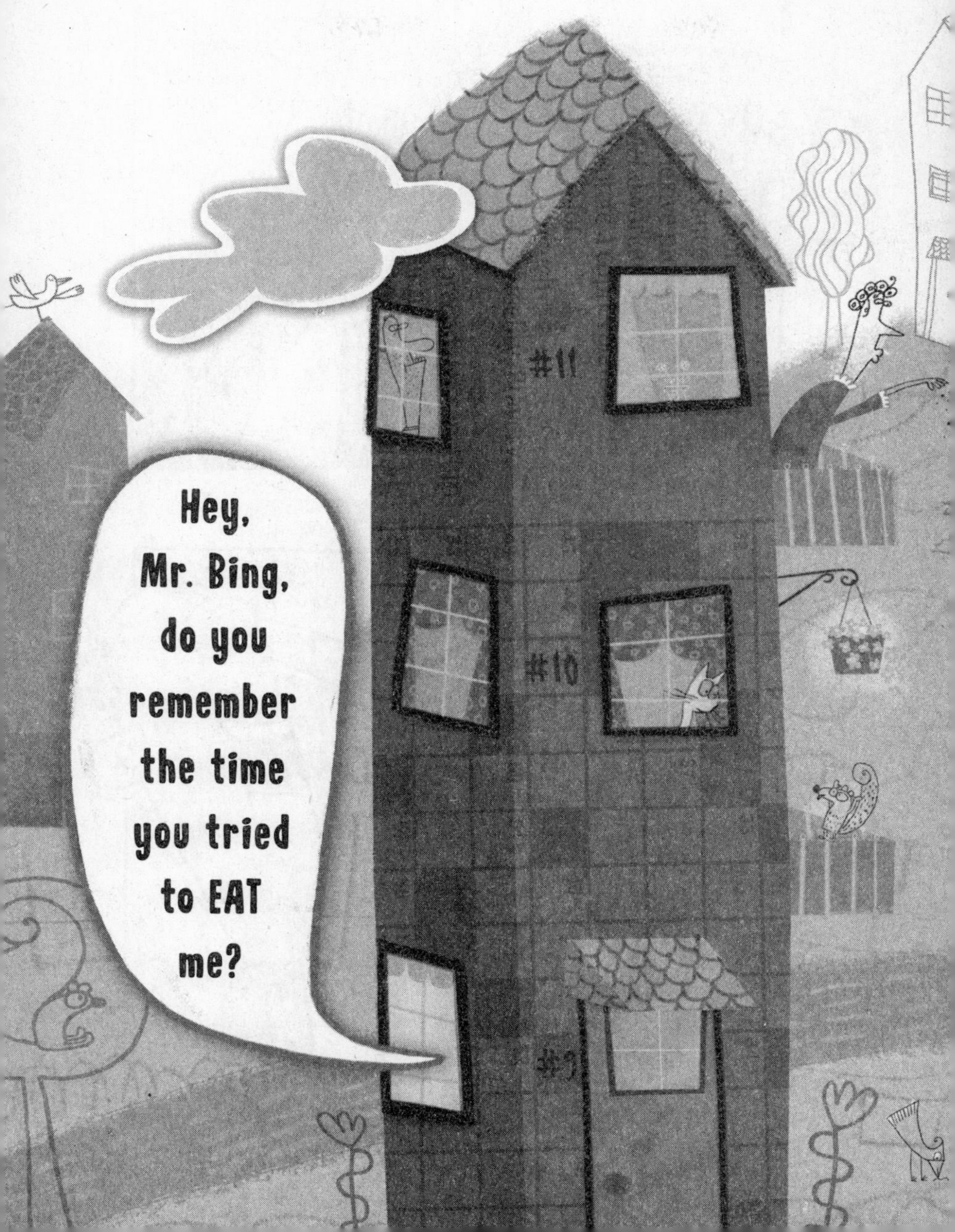

It seems like just yesterday that Mr. Bing brought me home from the Downtown Bakery and tried to eat me. Time sure flies. And look at us now—Mr. Bing and his trusty DOUGHNUT-DOG!

That's ME!

Adorable!

YUP, since Mr. Bing decided not to make me his **BREAKFAST** (phew!), he decided we should think of something **ELSE** he could make of me. Coming up with ideas was easy, but agreeing on one was **ANOTHER** story! I mean, would **YOU** want to be an **AIR FRESHENER** for someone's car?

Or a PICTURE FRAME?

And WHO in their right mind would want
to be a PINCUSHION?!

I guess I was hoping for something a *little* more glamorous.

Like being his **BALLROOM DANCE PARTNER**.

Or his **CHAUFFEUR**.

Or an **ENTERTAINER** at his parties.

"There's **NO** business like **DOUGH** business!"

Turns out he didn't like MY ideas any better than I liked HIS. We had given up trying and I was on my way out of town when Mr. Bing ran up to me with the doughnut-dog idea . . .

AND I LOVED IT!

But as popular as dogs are, we've discovered that some places don't like having dogs around—not even doughnut-dogs.

We've worked our way around it, though. Sometimes I'm a doughnut-dog.

And sometimes I'm just a *doughnut*.

A chocolate-covered sprinkle doughnut, that is!

But there's one thing that never changes— Mr. Bing and I are ALWAYS best friends.

CHAPTER 2

Mr. Bing LOVES to bowl. He and three of his friends are on a bowling league team called the BINGBATS. Tuesday is their league night, and Mr. Bing always lets me go with him to watch. I didn't think I'd like going to the bowling alley, but now Tuesday is my favorite night of the week!

MONDAY NIGHT — WOMEN'S LEAGUE
TUESDAY NIGHT — MEN'S LEAGUE
WEDNESDAY NIGHT — MIXED LEAGUE
THURSDAY NIGHT — ROBOT LEAGUE

Come down now, Arnie!

I like hanging out with the Bingbats.

Kenny

Bernie

Mr. Bing/Walter
(Team Captain)

Howard

Maybe it's because they all remind me of . . .

DOUGHNUTS!

Take BERNIE for instance. He's the classic GLAZED DOUGHNUT. He's popular and mellow and wears shiny "glaze" in his hair. And when he bowls, he slides on his shoe like it's coated with sugar.

Then there's HOWARD. He's the good ol' JELLY DOUGHNUT. He's sweet and jolly and when he rolls a strike, it makes the alley shake like a bowl full of jelly.

KENNY is the LONG JOHN of the group.

Pardon me, but I much prefer LONG JONATHAN, just as I'm sure Kenny prefers KENNETH.

He's tall and thin, and his bowling moves are as smooth as the creamy filling in a Long John.

And finally, MR. BING—he's the CINNAMON TWIST. He looks plain at first, but his personality has a surprising "spice" to it. And when he releases the ball, his arm does a little TWIST over his head.

I've made lots of **OTHER** friends at the bowling alley too. In fact, between the bowling balls, bowling pins, and rental shoes I've made

8 HOMIES,
11 PEEPS, and
13 BFFs!

They've taught me pretty much everything
I need to know about the game of bowling.

 **LIKE:**

* When a bowler knocks down all the pins
  in ONE try, it's called a **STRIKE**.

* When a bowler knocks down all the pins
  in TWO tries, it's called a **SPARE**.

* When a bowler doesn't knock down ANY
  pins, it's called a **GUTTER BALL**.

Oh, and the most important one:

* When a bowler takes off his smelly bowling
  shoes, **RUN FOR YOUR LIFE!**

P-U!

It's TRUE!
We STINK!

But of all the great things about the bowling alley, my favorite is that there's a restaurant inside called the BOWL-O'-CHOW and they have a KARAOKE MACHINE! I usually watch Mr. Bing bowl for a while, and then I wander over to the BOWL-O'-CHOW to sing a few songs. I was scared to try it at first, but now I'm a regular!

Here he is—the little doughnut who put the *O* in *KARAOKE*. Let's give it up for Arnie the Doughnut!

Woo Hoo!

Thanks, everybody!

Yay, Arnie!

Here are a few of my old standbys:

And I always end with my signature song:

CHAPTER 3

I'm not saying that I've never run into trouble at the bowling alley.

In case you're wondering if **I'M** a bowler . . .
I'm **NOT**. Doughnuts don't usually make
very good bowlers. It's a **SIZE** thing.

Help! I'm
a chocolate-
covered
sprinkle
pancake!

The average doughnut weighs only **1.8
ounces,** and the smallest bowling ball
weighs **6 pounds**.

+ = IMPOSSIBLE

But Mr. Bing is the **PERFECT** size for bowling. And he's gotten so good at it that this year he decided to buy his very **OWN** bowling ball.

Oh, that was ANOTHER one of Mr. Bing's ideas for me—to be his new BOWLING BALL!

In the past, Mr. Bing always used one of the bowling alley balls that anyone can use. His favorite was a 13-pounder named **BRUISER** from the wrong side of the racks (where the extra-rough-and-tough bowling balls live).

What's it TO ya, ERNIE?

He always calls me ERNIE!

But his new, purple bowling ball, **BETSY**, weighs a WHOPPING 15 POUNDS!

OH, NO!
Did I just say what I THINK I said?
Hold on, I can check that for you. ". . . doughnuts don't usually make very good bowlers . . ." Blah, blah, blah. ". . . the average doughnut weighs only 1.8 ounces. . . ." AH, here it is—"his new, purple bowling ball, Betsy, weighs a WHOPPING 15 POUNDS!" YEAH, you said it, all right.

HOLEY DOUGHNUT!

I just broke RULE #17 in the *Bowling Alley Rules and Regulations Handbook*:

RULE #17:
UNDER NO CIRCUMSTANCES SHALL ANYONE (not even cute little doughnuts) MENTION THE WEIGHT OF A FEMALE BOWLING BALL.

And that's exactly what I did. I blurted it out as casually as if I were saying that Mr. Bing owns a pair of pink, poodle boxing shorts!

Thanks for sharing that, Arnie!

Excusez-moi for interrupting, but Monsieur Arnie has made a big FAUX PAS (pronounced "FO-PAH"). It is the French word for, how you say, HE IS IN DEEP DOO-DOO.

(Le French Cruller)

Just wait till Betsy finds out. She'll have me banned from every bowling alley in the country!

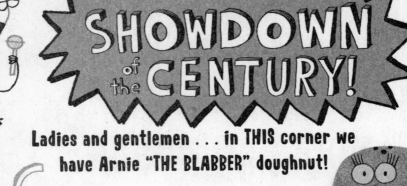

SHOWDOWN of the CENTURY!

Ladies and gentlemen . . . in THIS corner we have Arnie "THE BLABBER" doughnut!

And in THIS corner we have Betsy the "Let Him Have It" purple bowling ball!

It looks like Arnie is making the first move.

AMAZING! He actually APOLOGIZED to Betsy! Well, here's where she'll really let him have it!

UNBELIEVABLE!

She just told Arnie that she's **PROUD** of her 15 glorious pounds and she doesn't care **WHO** he tells!

They're actually **LAUGHING** about it!

Well, just when I thought I'd seen it all. It's looking like a **WIN-WIN** for this showdown tonight, folks!

CHAPTER 4

So tonight is a VERY

night for the Bingbats. They're competing
in the 62nd Annual Lemon Lanes Bowling
Championship! There are eight teams in
the men's league, and for the past six years

the Bingbats have finished in second place.
And for the past six years the team that
beat them is the **Yada-Yadas.**

Steamer
(Team Captain)

Bubba

Rupert

Frank

But **THIS** year the Bingbats have the
most points so far. If they can hang on to
their lead until the end of the night, that
FIRST-PLACE TROPHY will be theirs!

Since it's such an important night, I have a **BIG** surprise planned, and it involves one of my FAVORITE things to do—

SINGING!

I got the idea from going to a baseball game with Mr. Bing. (It was the same day I caught a fly ball. It stuck right to my frosting!)

During the seventh inning, the crowd stands to do the Seventh-Inning Stretch and sings "Take Me Out to the Ball Game" together:

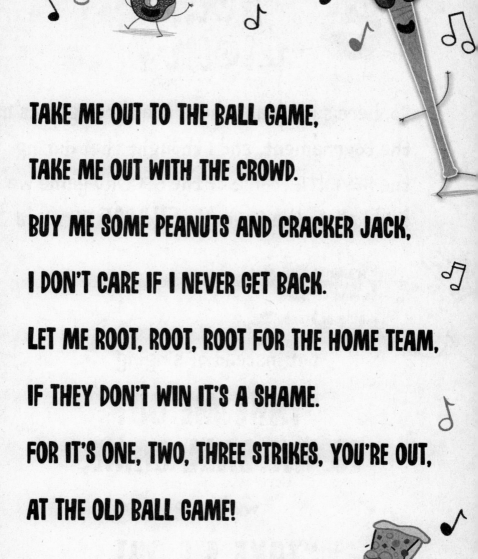

TAKE ME OUT TO THE BALL GAME,

TAKE ME OUT WITH THE CROWD.

BUY ME SOME PEANUTS AND CRACKER JACK,

I DON'T CARE IF I NEVER GET BACK.

LET ME ROOT, ROOT, ROOT FOR THE HOME TEAM,

IF THEY DON'T WIN IT'S A SHAME.

FOR IT'S ONE, TWO, THREE STRIKES, YOU'RE OUT,

AT THE OLD BALL GAME!

FUN, RIGHT?

So, here's my plan. There are three games in the tournament, and I thought that during the SEVENTH frame of the SECOND game we could all do the Seventh-FRAME Stretch!

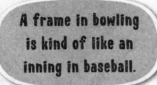

A frame in bowling is kind of like an inning in baseball.

But instead of singing

"TAKE ME OUT TO THE BALL GAME,"

we'll sing

"TAKE ME OUT FOR SOME BOWLING"!

I love it!

When I told Ms. Marlene, the manager at the BOWL-O'-CHOW about the Seventh-Frame Stretch, she suggested moving the karaoke machine out to the bowling alley so everyone could read the words on the big screen! I loved her idea, but I worried that the karaoke crowd would be upset about not being able to use it that night.

WHAT?!

NO KARAOKE TONIGHT?!

I've been practicing in the shower ALL WEEK!!!

Look, Grandma, that man is NAKED! And SOGGY!

Ms. Marlene said it wouldn't be a problem because on championship night everyone likes to watch the bowlers, so the restaurant is practically empty anyway. The only "bowling folks" who DIDN'T seem excited about the Seventh-Frame Stretch were the yada-yadas. In fact, they acted kind of GROUCHY when I told them.

Hey, Ernie, maybe the Yada-Yadas are grouchy because the Bingbats are in the lead and they're NOT.

Could Bruiser be RIGHT? Are the yada-yadas really grouchy because the Bingbats are in the lead and they're not? NOOOOOOO, that's RIDICULOUS!

I bet they were grouchy because their SHOES were too tight! They sure LOOKED tight.

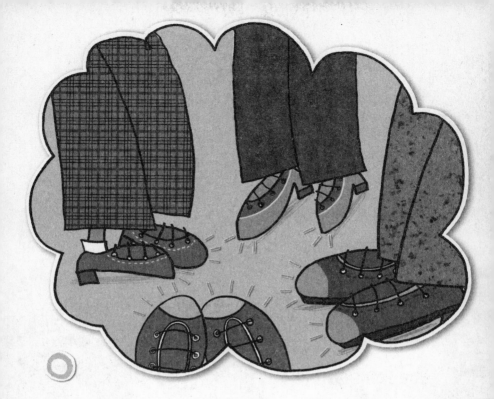

I tell ya, there aren't many things worse than shoes that are too tight. That's exactly why I don't wear them.

OH, THOSE POOR, GROUCHY YADA-YADAS AND THEIR ACHY FEET!

CHAPTER 5

We just arrived at the bowling alley, and this place is **HOPPING!**

BOWLING
$3.00 PER GAME
$2.00 SHOE RENTAL

EXIT

POP CORN

It reminds me of the morning I was made at the Downtown Bakery. The baker hung the **OPEN** sign in the window, and

The place was swarming with customers!

Enough reminiscing—it's time for some BOWLING! It's so exciting! But I have something to confess. While the Bingbats were busy putting on their bowling shoes, I dropped a few sprinkles in the thumbholes of their bowling balls. Not just ANY sprinkles, though. PINK sprinkles. Those are the LUCKY ones! I checked the rules and it's perfectly legal. So I figured a little good luck couldn't hurt on such a big night.

Between you and me, I'm glad he's using the PINK sprinkles. The BLUE ones make me so GASSY.

Now, I know it's early to be talking about trophies, but I want to show you my impersonation of the FIRST-PLACE TROPHY GUY.

PRETTY GOOD, RIGHT?

I don't see HOW he keeps his arms up like that all the time! If he comes home to live with us, I'm sure Mr. Bing would let him relax and put them down.

I'll bet Mr. Bing would even ask him to join us for dinner once in a while. BUT HE'D HAVE TO HELP WITH THE DISHES!

Please excuse me for just a minute. I need to run over to the bowling ball return. I like being there every few frames to welcome the bowling balls back. The bowling ball return sure looks like fun to ride on, but I hear it takes first-timers a while to get used to.

I've done it HUNDREDS of times and I'm still not used to it.

WELCOME BACK!
BARF BAGS AVAILABLE UPON REQUEST.

I don't think it would bother me, though.
I figure if I can make it through the Ringy
Dingy Doughnut-Making Thingy® without
getting sick, I can handle just about anything!

WHEEE!

RINGY DINGY DOUGHNUT-MAKING THINGY®

375°

All the teams are bowling really well, but the Bingbats are still in the lead. The pins must be loving all the strikes the bowlers have been getting—they're flying all over the place! So far I've seen them do

head spins, CORKscrews, and AiR CHAirs!*

I know that because the pins taught me some of the breakdancing moves they do once a bowling ball smashes into them. I've gotten pretty good, but I really need to be more careful. Last time I did it, they told me I **BUSTED A MOVE.**

Sorry, guys!

CHAPTER 6

The Bingbats won the first game! The second game is under way, and Mr. Bing just got his **THIRD STRIKE IN A ROW!**

STRIKE!

YAY, WALTER!

WOO-HOO!

Well, it's almost time for the Seventh-Frame Stretch, so I'd better head over to the karaoke machine to warm up my pipes.

I'm headed that way myself. Might you escort me?

But of course.

By any chance do you know the **TURKEY TROT?**

Why, it's my favorite trot!

In honor of tonight's tournament, Arnie the Doughnut will now lead us all in

THE SEVENTH-FRAME STRETCH!

So, please stand, stretch, and sing along to

"TAKE ME OUT FOR SOME BOWLING"!

That's my Arnie!

OH, I MISSED THE SPARE
ON THE FIFTH FRAME—
THAT GUTTER BALL WAS A SHAME.
BUT IT'S STRIKE, STRIKE,
NEXT TIME JUST STRIKES
FOR A PER-FECT GAME!

CHAPTER 7

Well, I haven't gotten the **OFFICIAL** word yet, but I'm getting the feeling that the Seventh-Frame Stretch was a **HIT!**

Encore!

Yay, Arnie!

I feel so refreshed!

WHAT?
A
TAP-DANCING
PIECE
OF
PIZZA?!
NOW
THIS
I'VE
GOTTA
SEE!

WHAT?
A
FIRE-EATING
FRENCH
FRY?!
NOW
THIS
I'VE
GOTTA
SEE!

Come on, let's go watch some bowling.

CHAPTER 8

Until this very moment, I thought finding out that doughnuts were made to be eaten was the only thing that could make my eyeballs do this:

It turns out that Mr. Bing throwing a GUTTER BALL makes them do that too!

POOR MR. BING!

In all the time I've known him, he's NEVER thrown a GUTTER BALL. What could have HAPPENED? Oh, I have to be quiet—he's about to finish the frame. I'm sure he'll get right back on track.

CHAPTER 9

Steamer, the captain of the yada-yadas, stole Betsy's lucky pink sprinkles?

So, Bruiser was RIGHT—the yada-yadas ARE upset because the Bingbats are in the lead. I noticed they didn't sing during the Seventh Frame Stretch. They just gave me grouchy looks and walked away—

TO STEAL THE LUCKY PINK SPRINKLES, THAT IS!

Now that the yada-yadas have the lucky pink sprinkles, **THEY'LL** have the extra good luck instead of the Bingbats. I have to get those sprinkles back without the yada-yadas knowing. But HOW?

I know, Arnie! We can make disguises from stuff in the Lost and Found so the Yada-Yadas won't recognize us. Then we can sneak over to their lane and steal back the lucky pink sprinkles!

GREAT IDEA, PEEZO!
I think that could work!

Why, HELLO THERE, SIR! How may we help you?
I need some small bandages.
Certainly, sir, we can get those for you.

No, we didn't take part in the Seventh-Frame Stretch because we have terrible singing voices and we didn't want to embarrass ourselves.
Then what's with all the grouchiness and dirty looks lately, huh?
The grouchiness and dirty looks are because of . . .

Well, I'm sorry for accusing you of stealing the lucky pink sprinkles. And I feel it's only fair for me to let you know we've been wearing disguises so you wouldn't recognize us. I'm really Mr. Bing's friend Arnie the Doughnut, and this is my friend Peezo.
WOW—you sure fooled me.
Now, WE'VE got some sprinkles to find and YOU'VE got to bandage up those disgusting feet and get back to bowling! Oh, and just so you know—in karaoke it doesn't matter HOW terrible you sing. EVERYONE is welcome!

CHAPTER 10

LEAPIN' LONG JOHNS!

Peezo and I were just walking past the bowling balls—the ones from the wrong side of the racks—and we overheard Rocky and Angus discussing something that stopped us in our tracks!

Hey, what's up with Bruiser painting himself purple?

I don't know, but he took off during that Seventh-Frame Stretch, mumbling something about getting back at that Bing guy and his new purple bowling ball.

I wonder if this has anything to do with the phone call I got from Bruiser the other day. I didn't think much of it at the time, but he sure had a lot of questions about the Seventh-Frame Stretch.

WAIT A MINUTE...

Bruiser always calls me ERNIE. When Betsy called me Ernie, I thought it was because she was confused after going into the gutter for the first time, but that wasn't the reason AT ALL.

She called me ERNIE because she's not Betsy—

SHE'S BRUISER!

All right, boys, you're on your own from here. I have to get back to the restaurant!

Ms. Marlene is the organ player?

So Bruiser painted himself purple to look like Betsy—but where's Betsy?

Look, Peezo—Bruiser's wet paint left a trail. It runs all the way down the gutter of Lane 24 at the end of the alley.

AHA!

That's why Bruiser asked about the Seventh-Frame Stretch. When everyone was singing, he rolled down the gutter and hid behind the lanes. Then he waited for Betsy to roll through, grabbed her, and took her place. And now he's rolling himself into the gutter every time Mr. Bing bowls! That means he's breaking Rule #61 in the *Bowling Alley Rules and Regulations Handbook*:

RULE #61:

A BOWLING BALL SHALL ONLY ROLL IN THE DIRECTION THAT A BOWLER ROLLS HIM OR HER.

I've got to get behind the lanes and follow Bruiser's paint trail so I can find Betsy and get her back into the game!

Okay, Peezo, on the count of three, give me a push!

ONE,

TWO,

THREE!

Bruiser's paint trail runs all the way behind Lane 10—the Bingbats' lane. This must be where he made the SWITCH!

LANE 10

HELP! I'm being BALL-NAPPED!

His trail keeps going,
but it's getting thinner!

OH, NO! Bruiser's paint
trail **RAN OUT** and Betsy's
nowhere around! How will
I ever find her **NOW?**

I don't know, but it looks like
you dropped one of your sprinkles
there, little doughnut guy.

No, I have
all 135.

WAIT!
That's one of the lucky
pink sprinkles I gave
to **BETSY!**

And there's another one!

And another one!

But where is the
last sprinkle?

PING!

OUCH!

BETSY!

She dropped her sprinkles so I could find her! BRILLIANT! But now I have to find a way to get her down. I wonder how Bruiser got her up there.

Hmmm mmmm mm mmm, mmm hmm mm hmm mm MMMM!

He used a ladder to get you up there but to make sure you didn't climb back down he gave it to a giant ladder-eating monster?

CHOMP! CHOMP! CHOMP! Mmmm, good ladder!

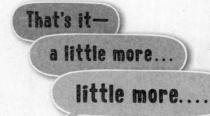

CHAPTER 12

Peezo just called and said
that Mr. Bing is still throwing
gutter balls and that the
Bingbats are now three points
BEHIND the yada-yadas!
There's one frame left, and
the only way the Bingbats can
win NOW is if Mr. Bing gets a
STRIKE. That way, he'll get
two BONUS ROLLS!

Come on, Betsy, we have
to catch Bruiser and get
you back in the game!

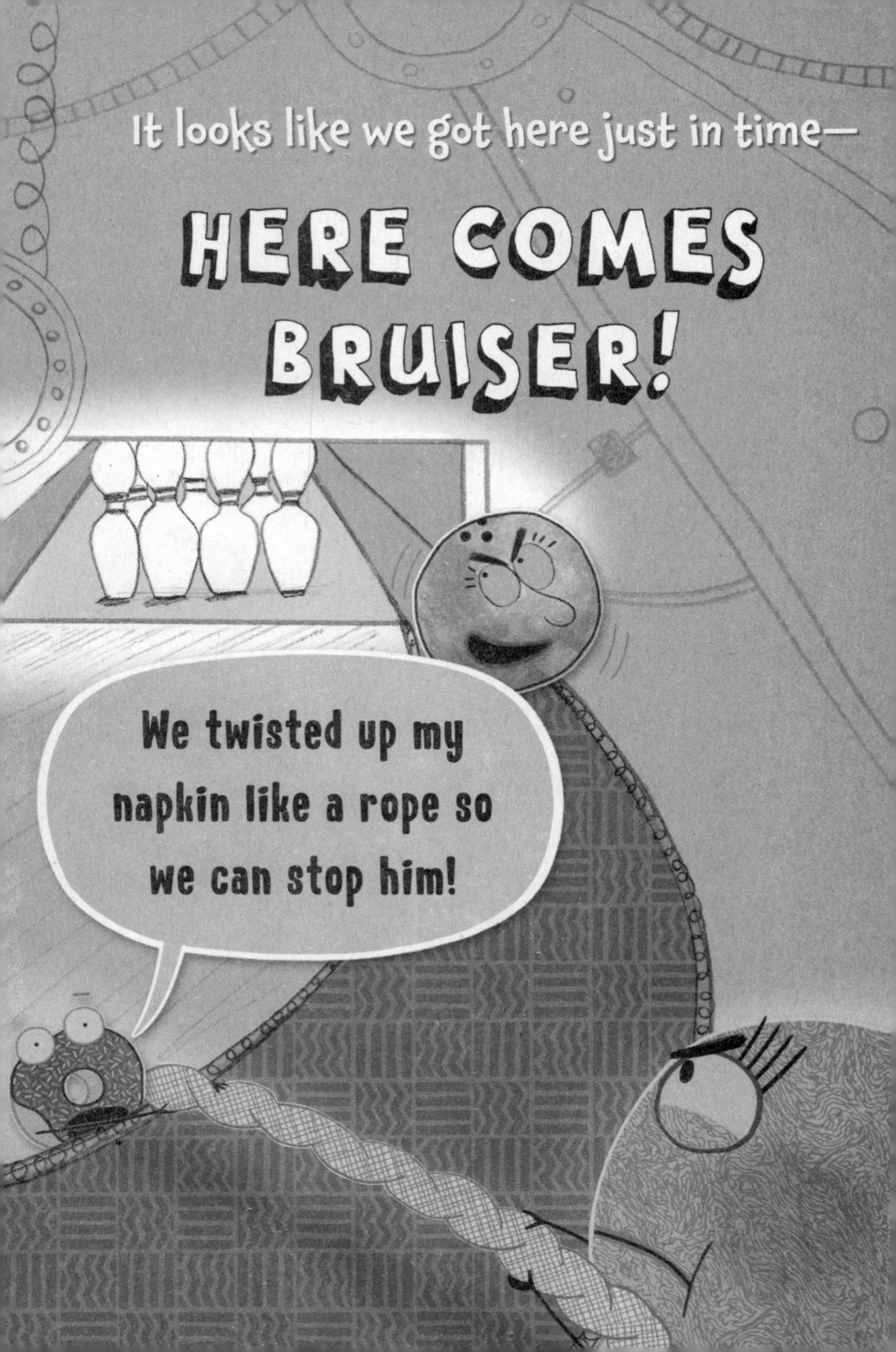
It looks like we got here just in time—
HERE COMES BRUISER!
We twisted up my napkin like a rope so we can stop him!

Nice try, Bruiser, but we're on to you! Now move over—it's time for the REAL Betsy to get back in the game!

Well, this is the moment of truth. Mr. Bing has to get a strike to get the bonus rolls. Now that Betsy's back with her lucky pink sprinkles, at least he stands a chance. Here he goes . . .

After all of Mr. Bing's gutter balls, he has to get a strike or a spare on the bonus rolls if the Bingbats are going to win the tournament.

On BONUS ROLL #1—

HE GOT AN 8!

And on BONUS ROLL #2—

The yada-yadas finished in second place. And no matter what Bruiser said, they don't seem upset about it at all.

Congratulations, Walter. Pardon my grouchy look—my shoes are killing me.

Thanks, Steamer.

That reminds me—
BRUISER.
I think we need to have a little talk.

CHAPTER 13

So, Bruiser—do you care to explain **WHY** you did what you did?

WELL?

I don't get it. You and Mr. Bing bowled together for years. How could you **DO** that to him?

How could I do that to **HIM?** How about what **HE** did to **ME**—dumping me for that fancy new bowling ball!

Excuse me, guys—I couldn't help overhearing.

Bruiser, you're a **LEMON LANES BOWLING BALL!** It's your job to help bowlers become so good that one day they'll buy their *OWN* bowling balls.

And that's what you did for Mr. Bing and lots of other bowlers. You're a **GREAT** bowling ball, Bruiser!

THAT'S THE MOST BEAUTIFUL THING I'VE EVER HEARD!

Come on, let's go to the party.

The party was off to a good start, but when Ms. Marlene said,

Hey, Arnie, KNOCK-KNOCK.

Who's there?

Kara.

Kara WHO?

KARAOKE TIME, EVERYONE!

that's when things REALLY got rollin'!

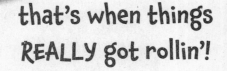

Everyone in the bowling alley sang at least one song—even the Yada-Yadas! Boy, they weren't kidding about their singing voices.

But even more shocking than that, Bruiser apologized to Betsy, **AND** they sang several songs together!

As the evening wound down, Mr. Bing and I each had one special THANK-YOU to make before we left the bowling alley.

Thanks, ol' Bruiser. I couldn't have won this without you.

Mr. Bing found the perfect place to put Stiffy Stu McShiny. That's what I call him because he won't tell me his name! Stiffy Stu seems a little shy, but I think he'll loosen up a bit once he's lived with us for a while.

Let's take him with us on our walk tomorrow, Mr. Bing!

I figured as soon as we got him home he'd finally put his arms down, but he hasn't ONCE! He can't fool me, though. I bet he puts them down as soon as the lights go out. Watch this. . . .

I'll wait thirty seconds and flip the lights back on. . . .

I'll wait a whole
minute this time....

I'll catch him tomorrow night for sure!

THE END

Turn the page for a peek at Arnie's NEXT adventure!

Go Fish!

GOFISH

LAURIE KELLER

What did you want to be when you grew up?
I remember wanting to be a TV weather person. I was fascinated with weather and liked watching David Compton report the weather on the local Channel 13 news!

When did you realize you wanted to be an illustrator?
Not until I was out of high school. I always loved art and took every art class available all through school, but I didn't realize I could do it as a job until I went with a friend to a student art exhibit at Kendall College of Art and Design. I enrolled there the following fall and got my degree in illustration. I worked for seven years as a greeting card artist for Hallmark before getting into children's books.

What's your most embarrassing childhood memory?
My skirt got stuck in a folding chair in choir practice, and when we were all supposed to stand and sing, I couldn't get up. The choir director was a very *gruff* sort, and when he saw me sitting, he pounded on the piano, stopped everyone from singing, and asked what I was doing. It was quite humiliating to explain. My face is turning red all over again just thinking about it!

As a young person, who did you look up to most?
My mom.

What was your first job, and what was your "worst" job?
My first job was selling fruit, pushing the cart around at a busy park. It also happened to be my worst job because on the first (and only) day, the manager stuffed ice down my shirt and later told me to call my mom and tell her she didn't have to pick me up because he could give me a ride home. Creepy! Of course I didn't do that. I told her what happened when she picked me up, and she made me quit. Smart mom.

How did you celebrate publishing your first book?
A very nice friend had a publishing party for me! I also celebrate whenever I finish a book by getting Chinese food.

Where do you work on your illustrations?
In my studio. Sometimes in the early sketch stages I sit outside, but most of the art is done inside at my desk.

Where do you find inspiration for your illustrations?
I have a huge collection of books that I like to thumb through, but lately I've been looking on Pinterest. I'm addicted!

What sparked your imagination for *Bowling Alley Bandit*?
Since I had already written a picture book about Arnie, I had some parameters set that helped me get started on choosing a scenario. I pored through the picture book to try to discover any anecdotes, characters, or "hidden" tidbits that might help me expand on Arnie's world. There's a section

where Arnie and Mr. Bing make lists of what Mr. Bing can do with Arnie instead of eating him. One of Mr. Bing's ideas was that Arnie could be his new bowling ball. And tucked back on Mr. Bing's bookshelf was a teeny second-place bowling trophy. That sealed the deal—I knew I had to do a bowling alley book! It was so much fun creating Mr. Bing's bowling teammates and all of Arnie's new bowling ball and bowling pin pals, and of course, his new favorite friend, Peezo (a greasy piece of bowling alley pizza no one ever bought).

What is your favorite thing about Arnie?
He's very adventurous and wants to get the most out of life.

What is your favorite kind of doughnut?
I've literally NEVER had a doughnut I don't like, but my favorite is the Krispy Kreme vanilla-filled, chocolate-covered doughnut. It kind of covers all the bases. I keep hearing how delicious Cronuts are, and I'm eager to try one! MMMMM . . . doughnuts (don't tell Arnie).

At the bowling alley, do you usually get all strikes or all gutter balls?
Certainly not all strikes! I don't go bowling very often, so I'm not a great bowler. I usually get a few strikes in a game, but I don't think I've ever scored over 150. I do think it's such a fun activity, though, and I love people-watching at the bowling alley. Everyone, for the most part, is having a good time!

What can readers look forward to in Arnie's next adventure, *Invasion of the Ufonuts*? No spoilers, please!
Arnie's town is in an uproar when a number of people claim they were abducted by alien doughnuts (Ufonuts)

from "outer spastry" (*pastry* and *space* combined). Everyone—except for Mr. Bing—is convinced that the Ufonuts are planning to take over Earth because they're upset that Earthlings eat doughnuts. Will Arnie be abducted, too? Hmmm . . . you'll have to read it to find out!

Where do you go for peace and quiet?
A walk by Lake Michigan or in the woods.

Who is your favorite fictional character?
If I had to pick just one, I'd choose Charlie Brown. He's so contemplative and kindhearted, and I love his tenacity despite living in a world that often disappoints him.

If you could travel in time, where would you go and what would you do?
I would zip back to the early 1500s and see if I could be Michelangelo's gofer as he painted the Sistine Chapel, for starters. I'm fascinated with that time period anyway, but to see him paint would be amazing.

What do you want readers to remember about your books?
Hopefully, that they had a laugh or two while reading them. One of my favorite things is when people tell me what lines in my books made them laugh. It doesn't get much better than that!

What would you do if you ever stopped illustrating?
If I were ever good enough, I'd love to be a banjo player in a bluegrass band. I've tinkered with the banjo on and off for years—mostly off, until recently. I take lessons again and

make time each day to practice. I also get together with some talented musician friends to play music. It makes me 100 percent happy!

Do you have any strange or funny habits? Did you when you were a kid?

If there are two items left on the shelf at a grocery store and I only need one, I have to buy both because it makes me feel too sad leaving the one by itself. I've been that way ever since I was little. I figured I'd grow out of it, but I think it's actually gotten worse!

As a kid, I didn't like uneven numbers. So when I would run scared up the stairs from the basement, I would step on the third step twice so it would make an even number of steps.

What do you wish you could do better?

Public speaking. I've always been terrified of it and used to avoid it at all costs. It's gotten easier for me over the years, but I'm by no means a natural at it. One thing that has helped is to set really low standards for myself: if I don't cry, faint, or vomit during a presentation, then I've knocked it out of the park! I really admire people who can get up in front of a large group and speak to them as though it's a room full of their best friends.

What would your readers be most surprised to learn about you?

How long it takes me to write my books. Once in a while they come together in a timely manner, but I second-guess myself again and again and again (and again and again), so it really slows down the process. I would love to be able to change that!

Who is your favorite artist?
If I had to pick one, I'd choose Delphine Durand.

What is your favorite medium to work in?
Acrylic paint and collage.

What was your favorite book or comic/graphic novel when you were a kid? What's your current favorite?
Nancy was my most favorite comic book as a kid, followed by *Richie Rich* and *Little Lulu*. These are probably hybrid graphic novel/chapter books, but I really like *Diary of a Wimpy Kid, Captain Underpants,* and *Dear Dumb Diary.* Janet Tashjian's My Life books are very entertaining. The Just Grace books by Charise Mericle Harper have elements of a graphic novel in them, and I think they're spectacular.

What challenges do you face in the artistic process, and how do you overcome them?
I can easily make my illustrations too busy and cluttered. Sometimes it works okay, but many times I have to go back in and simplify them.

If you could travel anywhere in the world, where would you go and what would you do?
I've traveled quite a bit around the world, but the place I most want to go is Alaska. I'd camp and hike and soak up the great outdoors. Maybe have tea with a grizzly bear?

Arnie is headed to outer space for some alien doughnut adventures!

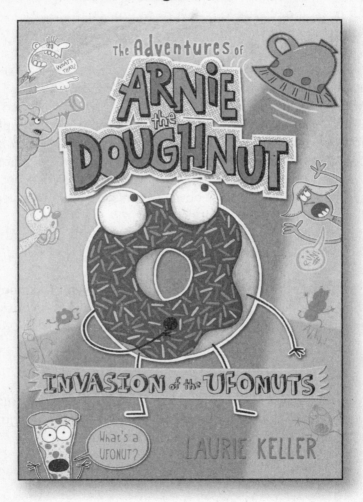

Will Arnie be abducted?!
Keep reading for a sneak peek!

The newspeople aren't interviewing Queenie LaTaffy or *ANY* famous person—they're interviewing my neighbor, Loretta Schmoretta! I wonder what's going on.

Folks, it looks like we've got a real outer space—or in THIS case, outer SPASTRY—story on our hands. Loretta Schmoretta is the sixteenth person today claiming to have been abducted by alien doughnuts, then released after the aliens stole their Downtown Bakery doughnuts! Tell us more, Loretta.

Okay.

Well, I was walking through the parking lot to my apartment with my bag of DOWNTOWN BAKERY doughnuts when I heard a LOUD CLINKING noise overhead. I looked up and saw a FLYING SAUCER floating above me! Actually, it was a flying CUP and saucer. I tried to run but a glowing beam of green, sticky jelly stopped me in my tracks. SUDDENLY I was inside the spacecraft, surrounded by gigantic DOUGHNUT CREATURES! There must have been a DOZEN of them!

They kept staring at me and mumbling to one another. I couldn't understand a word they said. They just stared and mumbled.

STARED AND MUMBLED.

STARED AND MUMBLED.

STARED AND MUMBLED

Yeah, we get it. THEN what happened?

Then they grabbed my doughnuts, and next thing I knew I was back on the ground. I saw them fly off and I haven't seen them since!

Loretta Schmoretta, why do you think the aliens are abducting Earthling doughnuts? Do you think they're rescuing them before they come back to take over Earth?
Oh, dear. I hadn't thought of *THAT*. I bet you're right.

Well, you heard it HERE, folks—ALIEN DOUGHNUTS FROM OUTER SPASTRY ARE PLANNING TO TAKE OVER EARTH BECAUSE WE EAT DOUGHNUTS!